Disney's DOGS

EDITIONS

New York

AN IMPRINT OF DISNEY BOOK GROUP

Original "Disney Unleashed" Concept by the Animation Research Library
a division of the Walt Disney Animation Studios

Published by Disney Editions, an imprint of Disney Book Group.

Book Concept and Design by
Tamara Khalaf

Disney Editions
Wendy Lefkon, Editorial Director
Jody Revenson, Senior Editor
Jessica Ward, Assistant Editor

For information address:
Disney Editions
114 Fifth Avenue
New York, New York 10011-5690

Library of Congress Cataloging-in-Publication data on file
ISBN 978-14231-0920-4

Printed in Singapore

CONTENTS

INTRODUCTION

Walt, his wife, Lilly, and their chow, Sunnee

Rex and Tom . . . Prince and Rollo . . . Buck and Sheila. . . Salty and Pepper and Lucy . . . oh, wait—those were all my real dogs. They were Disney dogs, too, but none of them wound up in the movies.

This book is about all those other dogs I grew up and spent most of my life with—the animated ones, from Pluto to Pongo, from Tramp to Bolt . . . and not to forget Goofy, who started out life with another name: Dippy Dawg.

The relationship between dogs and their people is as old as civilization. And from time immemorial, we have watched our dogs, and wondered what they were thinking. The Disney artists not only knew what they were thinking, they found a thousand ways to put pencil to paper and tell us.

Left: Walt with Duchess
Above: Walt and his uncle Robert, filming the family dog

Of course, over time, the Disney dogs grew even more sophisticated and more human—they could talk, and reason, and plot, and scheme, and express every possible emotion through their (animated) body language.

But they never crossed the line. They never turned into humans. They were always dogs, and I think they only made us love our real dogs more.

I hope you will enjoy this wonderful collection of drawings. They bring a whole new meaning to the phrase, "Man's Best Friend."

Roy E. Disney
 Vice Chairman Emeritus, The Walt Disney
 Company, and Dog Lover

Walt at his home with his poodle, Lady

Walt reviews a script with trusty companion

Roy E. Disney and Lucy

CHAPTER ONE
OLD DOGS, NEW TRICKS

Disney Dogs from the early short films

Make no bones about it—these old dogs have certainly earned their place in the heart of many a Disney dog lover. Perhaps the best known of these dogs from the early years is Pluto, Mickey's fun-loving pet. His first appearance with Mickey Mouse was in *The Chain Gang* (1930), where he was unnamed. It wasn't until a year later that he debuted as Pluto in *The Moose Hunt* (1931).

Since then, Pluto has become synonymous with loyalty, curiosity, protection, and playful devotion. His exemplary bravery in *Society Dog Show* (1939) and other shorts turned him into a national symbol of patriotism, and Pluto's image appeared on approximately forty-five military insignias during World War II. Aside from Pluto's circle—which includes his pup (Pluto, Jr.), two girlfriends (Dinah and Fifi), and arch-nemesis (Butch)—there is an equally unique group of old dogs whose playfulness, mischief, and affection make them as diverse as the many breeds of dogs themselves.

10

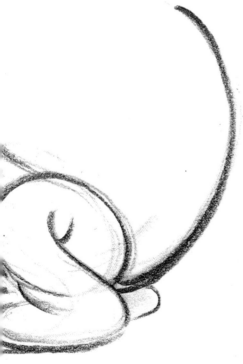

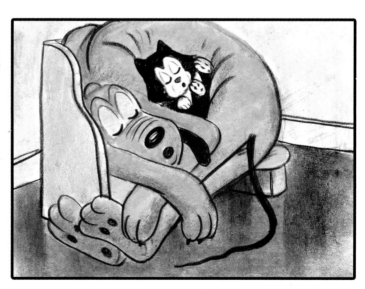

SCENE 5

SCENE 5

M.L.S. - Minnie tastes batter, exits.
Fly enters scene.

SCENE 5.1

C.U. - Fifi watches fly, makes
take.

SCENE 4

C.U. Fifi - listen-
ing to Minnie o.s.
"... HIS MOTHER
USED TO MAKE."

SCENE 22

PLUTO AND FIFI RUB NOSES.

"RONNIE"
10,000 BONES RANSOM ASKED FOR BABY PUP.

"PLUTO"
"ROOKIE" POLICE DOG ON TRAIL OF MISSING PUP.

"BUTCH"
PAROLED DOGNAPPER SEEN IN VICINITY

Some days you're the dog, some days you're the hydrant.

— Anonymous

23

The dog represents all
that is best in man.

— Etienne Charlet

31

A dog wags
his tail
with his
heart.

— Martin Buxbaum

40

When a dog wags its tail and barks at the same time, how do you know which end to believe?

— Anonymous

CHAPTER TWO
HOT DOGS

Disney Dogs starring in feature film roles

The role of the canine in Disney's films expanded in the 1950s from adorable pets to talking-and-thinking heroes. Told from the point of view of these four-legged friends, these movies captured the evolving and integral role of the canine both in society and in film.

The soaring popularity of dogs in our culture led Disney animators to create stories with all-dog casts. The first to appear was *Lady and the Tramp* (1955), the Studios' first feature film not based on a published novel or story. Soon to follow was another film with an all-canine cast. Here's a hint: what has 6,469,952 spots? That's the total number of spots that appear in the stylized production of *One Hundred and One Dalmatians* (1961). And to prove that animators weren't barking up the wrong tree by featuring canines in lead roles, films such as *The Fox and the Hound* (1981) and *Oliver & Company* (1988) proved that these formidable pups are all top dogs.

Money will buy you a pretty good dog, but it won't buy the wag of his tail.

— Henry Wheeler Shaw

A house is not a home without a dog in it.

— Anonymous

"PUPPIES"
Prod. 2110

PEPPER

ROLLY

OK Ken

"LUCKY"

PATCH

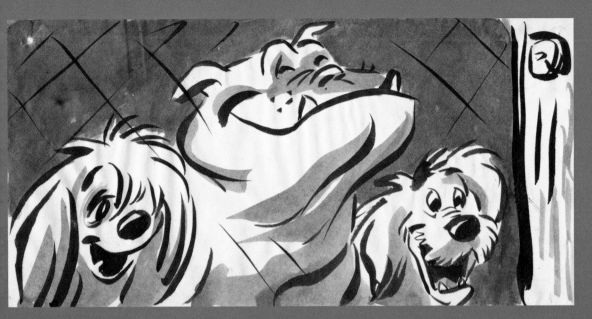

To err is human, to forgive, canine.

— Anonymous

the TRAMP
PROD. 2079

OK GERONIMI
HAM LUSKE

OK JAXON

My little dog—a heartbeat at my feet.

— Edith Wharton

My goal in life is to be as good a person as my dog already thinks I am.

— Anonymous

81

Oliver &

Size Comparison Sheet

GEORGETTE   FRANCIS TITO EINSTEIN

Company

Production # 0421

DODGER   OLIVER   RITA   THE DOBERBOYS

GEORGETTE

EYE CIRCLE
INS. BOW   LIDS

BAL. BOW

                            BAL. COLLAR
                            EDGE OF COLLAR

              FUR

BODY   FUR SHADOW

CHAPTER THREE
THEIR BARK IS BIGGER THAN THEIR BITE

Disney Dogs in Supporting Roles

In time, Disney dogs seemed to reach a level of enlightenment, possessing more humanlike attributes than their real-life counterparts. These dogs proved they were more than mere pets. They were capable of solving mysteries, protecting children, serving as town sheriffs, and, especially, saving the day!

Many Disney films would be less memorable were it not for characters such as the Darlings' nanny-dog, Nana, in *Peter Pan* (1953); Basil and Dawson's clever companion, Toby, in *The Great Mouse Detective* (1986); or the spoiled Percy from *Pocahontas* (1995). In this dog-eat-dog world, every dog must have its day—even if it is in a supporting role.

MRS DARLING HUMS A PHRASE

Our perfect companions never have fewer than four feet. — Colette

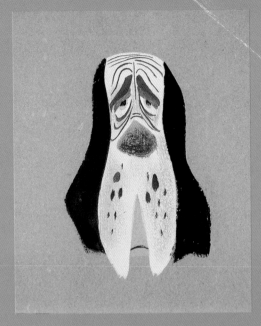

One reason a dog is such comfort when you're down-cast is that he doesn't ask to know why.

— Anonymous

Y ou do not own a dog,
the dog owns you.

— Anonymous

A TIBETAN
PRAYER DOG

BASED ON
CHRIST SANDERS
SKETCH

113

D ogs are not our whole life, but they make our lives whole.

— Roger Caras

The totality of all questions and all answers is contained in the dog.
— Franz Kafka

121

CHAPTER FOUR
OFF THE LEASH

Untraditional Disney Dogs

"Is he or isn't he?" That question is asked a lot. Is Goofy a dog? Well, it's best to say that he's that friend of Mickey's with the doglike features. Originating from bit parts in early short films, Goofy soon became one of the "Fab Five," serving as the humorous and dim-witted friend with a propensity toward chaotic mishaps. Beyond Goofy, Disney animators took our passion for dogs one step further and defied the conventional definition of the word dog, by transferring the best pooch qualities into anthropo-morphized objects. From the enchanted footstools in *Beauty and the Beast* (1991) and *Thru the Mirror* (1936), to the toylike Slinky Dog in *Toy Story* (1995) and the animated bone-dog, Zero, from *Tim Burton's The Nightmare Before Christmas* (1993), to Stitch, the alien disguised as a dog in *Lilo & Stitch* (2002), these untraditional dogs pack a bite that may make their real dog counterparts want to "flea."

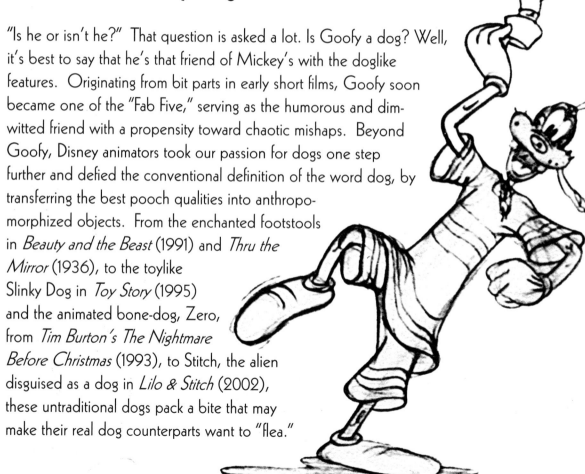

The
GOOF

MOUTHFULL

"OUCH!"

GOOFY HERO
THE SPORT

HAT APPR.
I HEAD
HIGH

HEAVY
UNDER
LIP

SNOUT BEGINS
APPR. 1/3 UP
ON HEAD

KNEES BREAK
BELOW CENTER
TO HELP GIVE
SLOUCH TO
BODY

E very dog must have his day.

— Jonathan Swift

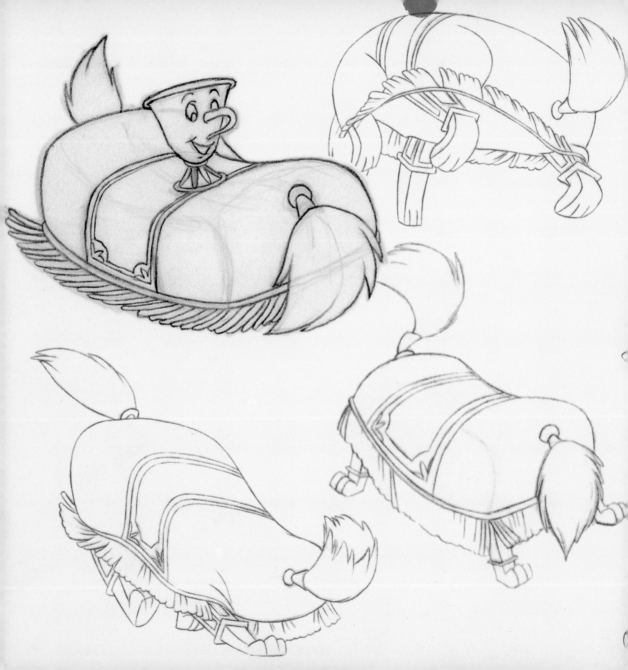

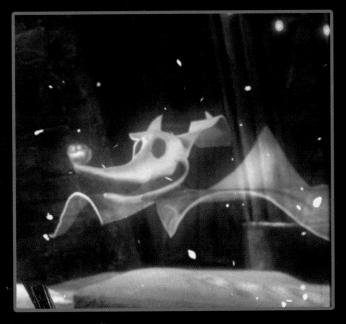

W hen you feel dog tired at night,
it may be because you've
growled all day long.

— Anonymous

One reason a dog is such a lovable creature is his tail wags instead of his tongue.

— Anonymous

CHAPTER FIVE
BOLT

New four-legged American hero

For superdog Bolt, every day is filled with adventure, danger, and intrigue—at least until the cameras stop rolling. When the star of a hit TV show is accidentally shipped from his Hollywood soundstage to New York City, he begins his biggest adventure yet—a cross-country journey through the real world. Armed only with the delusion that all his amazing feats and powers are real, and with the help of two unlikely traveling companions——a jaded, abandoned housecat named Mittens and a TV-obsessed, plastic-ball-dwelling hamster named Rhino—Bolt discovers he doesn't need superpowers to be a hero.

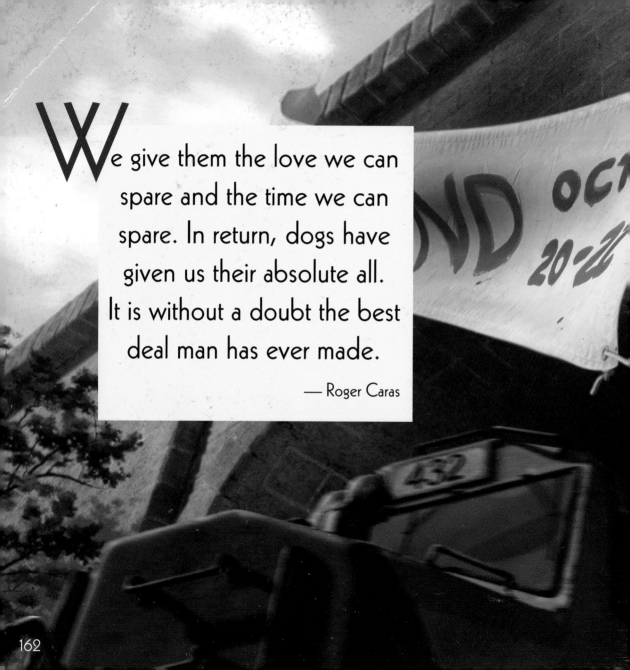

We give them the love we can spare and the time we can spare. In return, dogs have given us their absolute all. It is without a doubt the best deal man has ever made.

— Roger Caras

FLIP BOOKS

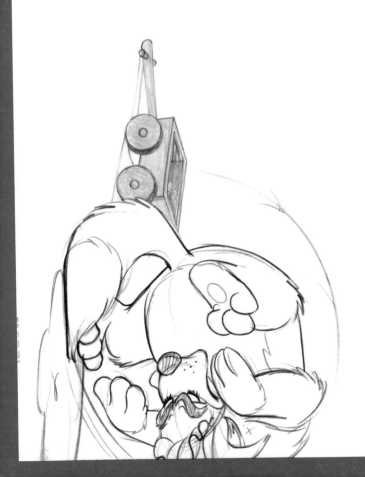

FLIP BOOKS

FLIP BOOKS

FLIP BOOKS

FLIP BOOKS

FLIP BOOKS

FLIP BOOKS

FLIP BOOKS

FLIP BOOKS

FLIP BOOKS

FLIP BOOKS

FLIP BOOKS

FLIP BOOKS

FLIP BOOKS

FLIP BOOKS

FLIP BOOKS

CANDY 9

RUBYS

CANDY 3
CANDY 3
MUSTARD 2
MUSTARD ½

FLIP BOOKS

FLIP BOOKS

LIST OF ILLUSTRATIONS

ACKNOWLEDGMENTS

To the talented artists whose work graces these pages, we thank you for bringing these characters to life through your drawings and animation. You have captured the spirit, loyalty, and charm of our canine friends by making us cry, love, and perhaps even howl, at life.
We are all the richer because of it.

For their contributions in creativity, ideas, and endless dog puns, special thanks go to Jody Revenson and Timothy Palin.

This book would not be possible without the unflagging efforts of a very talented staff at the Disney Animation Research Library. Thanks specifically to Ann Hansen and Fox Carney for chasing down obscure images and giving me options too numerous to count. The hardest part was selecting the best ones!

An equally generous thanks goes to directors Lella Smith and Mary Walsh, and the rest of the ARL gang: Tammy Crosson, Doug Engalla, Kerry Kugelman, Daryl Maxwell, Kristen McCormick, Scott Pereira, Jackie Vasquez, Darryl Vonture, and Patrick White.

Additional thanks for contributions to: Renato Latanzi, Kent Gordon, Clark Spencer, LeighAnna McFadden, Hugh Chitwood, Vivian Procopio, and Connie Thompson.

This book is dedicated to dog lovers of all sizes and breeds, and to the magnificent Maltese who left a paw print on my heart, Misty Khalaf.